C 4

j567.97 Simon, Seymour.
S
        The largest
        dinosaurs

$10.95

DATE		
JAN 1 9 1988	MAR 3 0 1989	MAY 1 9 1994
FEB 0 9 1988	JUL 1 9 1989	AUG 1 8 1994
APR 2 0 1988	NOV 3 1989	NOV 1 0 1994
		FEB 0 2 1995
AUG 0 3 1988	JAN 0 4 1990	FEB 2 8 1995
		JUN 3 0 1995
	FEB 0 8 1990	MAR 1 5 1996
AUG 3 0 1988	APR 1 3 1990	MAY 2 7 1997
SEP 0 2 1988	MAY 3 0 1990	NOV 0 4 1997
SEP 2 2 1988	AUG 3 0 1991	FEB 2 3 1999
	APR 0 9 1992	AUG 2 4 1999
JAN 2 6 1989	MAY 1 8 1993	

The Largest Dinosaurs

Seymour Simon
illustrated by Pamela Carroll

Macmillan Publishing Company
New York
Collier Macmillan Publishers
London

Macmillan Publishing Company
866 Third Avenue, New York, NY 10022
Collier Macmillan Canada, Inc.

Printed in the United States of America

10 9 8 7 6 5 4 3 2 1

The text of this book is set in 12 pt. ITC Bookman.
The illustrations are rendered in ink line and stippling
with watercolor wash.

Library of Congress Cataloging-in-Publication Data
Simon, Seymour.
The largest dinosaurs.
Includes index.
Summary: Surveys findings on Brachiosaurus,
Diplodocus, and four other examples of the largest
dinosaurs, including the locations of the discoveries
and explanations of their names.
1. Dinosaurs—Juvenile literature. [1. Dinosaurs]
I. Carroll, Pamela, ill. II. Title.
QE862.D5S52   1986   567.9'1   85-24088
ISBN 0-02-782910-3

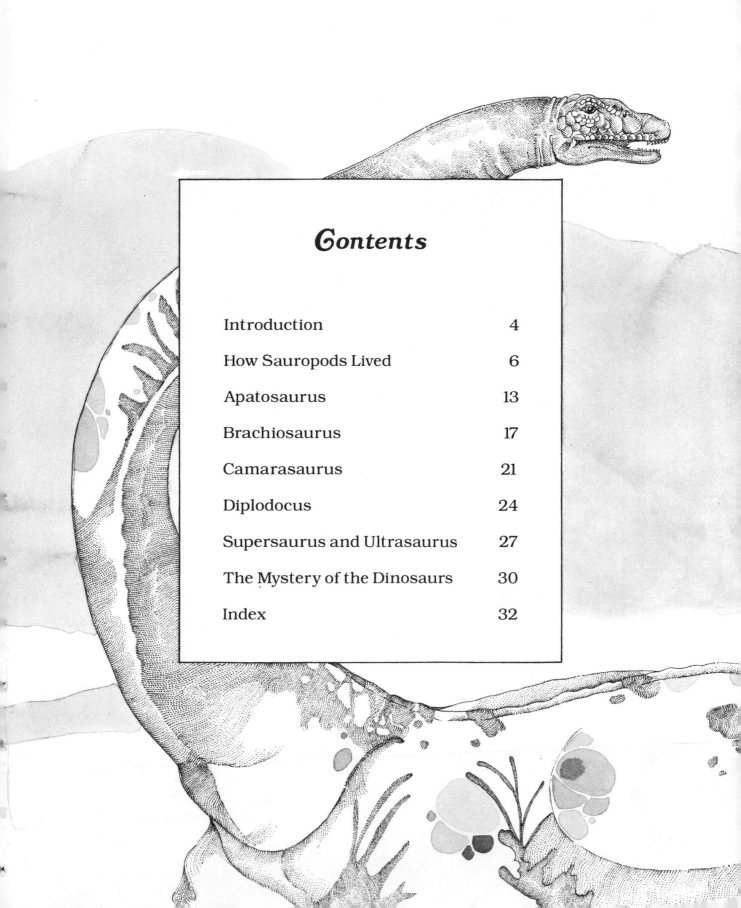

Contents

Introduction

Some dinosaurs were giants. These giant dinosaurs weighed more than a heavy cement truck. They were longer than your school lunchroom. They were taller than an apple tree.

The largest of all the dinosaurs belong to a family named Sauropods, which means "lizard feet." They were given that name because their feet looked the way lizards' feet do today. There were other large dinosaurs, but none were as large as some of the sauropods.

A sauropod's body was very large. Each of its four legs was as thick as a tree trunk. Its leg bones were very strong and heavy. But its backbones were hollow and very light in weight.

Sauropods had small heads and long necks and tails. With their long necks, they could raise their heads high above the ground. Some of these giant dinosaurs had heads smaller than a horse's and brains no larger than a kitten's. Sauropods had small brains for such large bodies.

All sauropods ate plants. They did not eat other animals. Sauropods lived for millions of years in North America, Africa, and China. This book is about these large dinosaurs. It tells how they lived in their surroundings and how they used their size to survive.

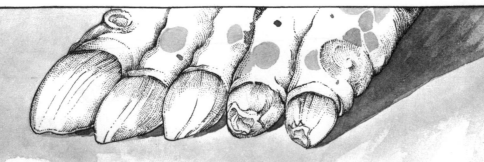

# How Sauropods Lived

(SAW–ruh–pods)

Scientists are not exactly sure how sauropods lived. That's because no one has ever seen a real sauropod. The last sauropods died many years before people lived on Earth.

But the sauropods left clues to what they were like. Some of the clues are *fossils.* Bones that change to rock are called fossils. Other clues are tracks in mud that hardened into rock. Scientists have also found hardened sauropod eggs and nests.

Scientists look closely at the clues they find. They think about the clues and form ideas about the way these dinosaurs looked and lived. Sometimes they change their ideas.

At one time, scientists believed sauropods lived in shallow water in lakes. They thought the water helped support the weight of their heavy bodies. But now, scientists believe that sauropods lived mostly on dry land.

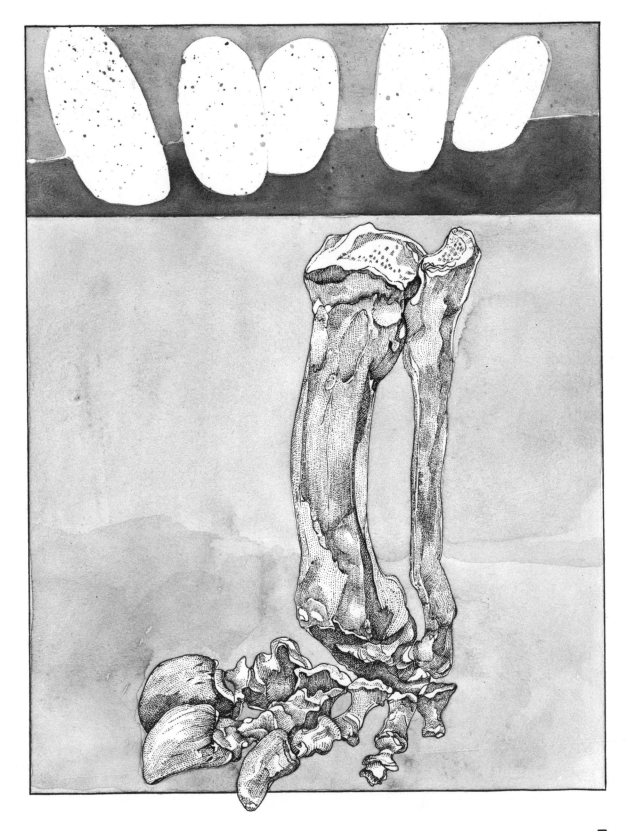

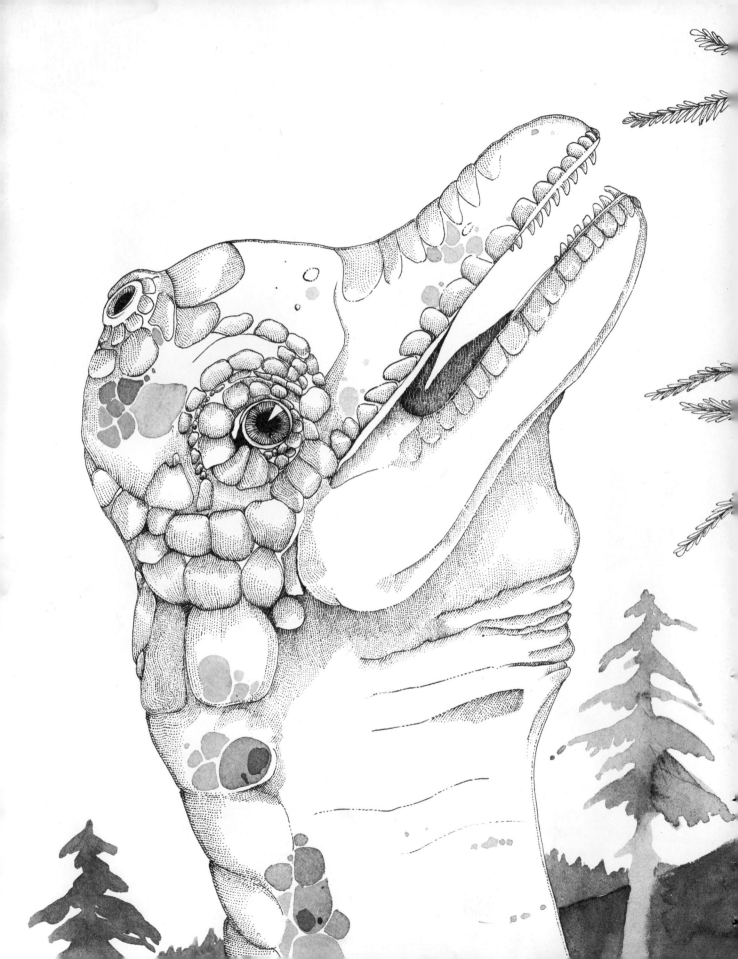

The sauropods probably used their long necks to reach tender leaves high up on trees. Some sauropods had only a few weak teeth to chew the leaves. They swallowed the leaves nearly whole.

The sauropods also swallowed rough stones about the size of your fist. The stones are called *gastroliths.* The stones rubbed against the leaves in a sauropod's stomach. The leaves were ground to a small size. The stones helped the sauropods to digest their food. In time, the stones were ground smooth. Scientists have found thousands of these stones mixed with dinosaur fossils.

The giant sauropods were big eaters. They ate all the leaves off nearby trees. Then they looked for more food. Their tracks show that the sauropods moved in herds. The herds moved across a land covered by tall trees. The tracks also show that the young sauropods traveled in the middle of the herds, where they were protected from danger.

Sauropods were dinosaurs, and all dinosaurs hatch from eggs. But some scientists think that sauropods may have been

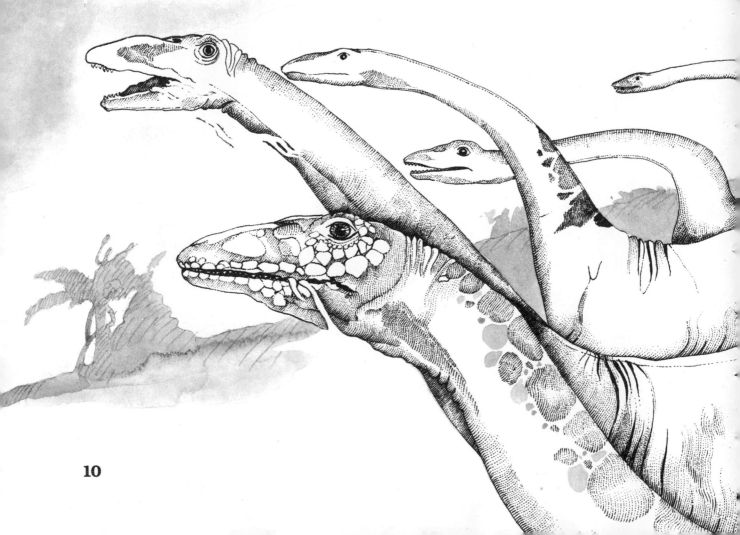

born alive, from eggs that were kept within the mother's body. The young sauropods may have moved with the herds from birth.

The six sauropods in this book are just a few of the many kinds whose fossil bones have been found. These six were chosen because they are among the biggest and best known. Many of the other sauropods were much the same as the ones in this book. But some may have lived differently.

 # *Apatosaurus*

(ah–PAT–uh–saw–rus)

Apatosaurus is a familiar-looking dinosaur with an unfamiliar name. Its name means "deceptive lizard." You probably know this dinosaur by another name. It is also called Brontosaurus, which means "thunder lizard." It was called that because of the way it was supposed to make the ground shake as it walked.

Apatosaurus was about seventy feet long and weighed thirty-five tons. That's longer than a big bus and as heavy as twenty cars.

Skeletons of Apatosaurus are in several museums in the United States, but, until a few years ago, the museums had the wrong skull on display. It belonged to a different kind of dinosaur. Many books and pictures still show the wrong shape. It was not until 1979 that a true Apatosaurus skull was found.

The shape of the true skull was much different from the other one on the museums' skeletons. Apatosaurus really had a flat head, about as large as a horse's, with a long snout. The head was small for its body. It had small, pencil-like teeth at the front of its jaws. It ate leaves and tender shoots from the tops of tall evergreen trees.

Apatosaurus had a twenty-foot-long neck and an even longer tail. Each of its legs looked like an elephant's, round and sturdy. Apatosaurus had large eyes and could probably see, hear, and smell very well. These sharp senses helped it to find food and avoid dangerous animals.

Large, meat-eating dinosaurs hunted Apatosaurus. For defense, Apatosaurus relied on its size, its thick skin, and its tail, with which it lashed out at attackers. Apatosaurus probably also traveled in herds for protection.

Apatosaurus probably spent most of the time on land but sometimes waded in rivers and lakes. Apatosaurus lived in the western part of the United States.

Brachiosaurus

(BRACK–ee–uh–saw–rus)

Brachiosaurus was one of the largest animals that ever lived. It had a long neck, high shoulders, and very long front legs, or "arms." Its name means "arm lizard."

Brachiosaurus was more than seventy-five feet long. That's probably farther than you can throw a ball. It had a thick tail, shoulders as high as a telephone pole, and a fairly small head atop a very long neck. By lifting its long neck, it could raise its head as high as a four-story building. It browsed on leaves high among the treetops. Brachiosaurus had to eat many leaves to fill its huge stomach.

Scientists once thought that Brachiosaurus lived mostly in deep-water lakes. They thought that only its head showed above the water. But scientists now think that Brachiosaurus lived most of its life on land. They think that this giant animal would not have been able to breathe if its body had been so far below the surface. The pressure of the water would have prevented its lungs from moving in and out.

Brachiosaurus probably did eat water plants and wade in shallow water from time to time. But lakes were dangerous places. Giant crocodiles easily could have drowned a sauropod by gripping its neck and holding its head below the water. It was safer for Brachiosaurus to live on land. Its huge size and tough skin protected it from most meat-eating dinosaurs.

Brachiosaurus fossils have been found in Colorado, Algeria, and Tanzania.

Camarasaurus

(KAM–uh–ruh–saw–rus)

Camarasaurus was the most common sauropod of its time. Its name means "chambered lizard." The "chambers" are hollow spaces in its backbone.

Camarasaurus had a short, sturdy body, a long neck, and a long tail. It measured between forty and sixty feet from the tip of its nose to the tip of its tail.

Camarasaurus looked different from most other sauropods. Most sauropods seem to slope backward. But Camarasaurus's front legs were nearly as long as its hind ones. That made its back seem to be straight across. Camarasaurus ate the leaves of plants that grew close to the ground.

Camarasaurus's skull was large, and it had big eyes. Its face was short and deep. Dozens of three-inch, pencil-like teeth rimmed its jaws. The skull mistakenly put atop an Apatosaurus skeleton was that of a Camarasaurus.

Many fossils of young Camarasaurus have been found. One such fossilized skeleton was found in Utah. The young dinosaur was sixteen feet long and shaped differently from the adult Camarasaurus. At first, scientists thought it was a completely different dinosaur. They even gave it another name. But further study convinced them that it was the same

kind of sauropod as the adult Camarasaurus. The young Camarasaurus had a larger head and a much shorter neck and tail, in proportion to its size, than did the adult.

Camarasaurus traveled in herds. Their fossils have been found in Colorado, Oklahoma, and Wyoming, as well as in Utah.

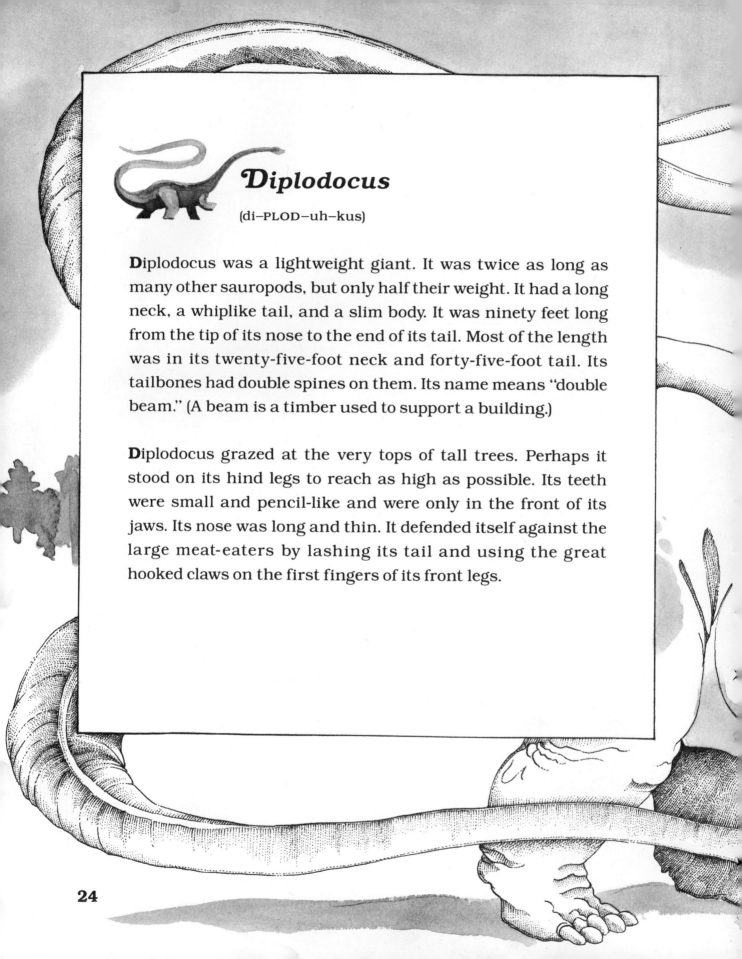

Diplodocus

(di–PLOD–uh–kus)

Diplodocus was a lightweight giant. It was twice as long as many other sauropods, but only half their weight. It had a long neck, a whiplike tail, and a slim body. It was ninety feet long from the tip of its nose to the end of its tail. Most of the length was in its twenty-five-foot neck and forty-five-foot tail. Its tailbones had double spines on them. Its name means "double beam." (A beam is a timber used to support a building.)

Diplodocus grazed at the very tops of tall trees. Perhaps it stood on its hind legs to reach as high as possible. Its teeth were small and pencil-like and were only in the front of its jaws. Its nose was long and thin. It defended itself against the large meat-eaters by lashing its tail and using the great hooked claws on the first fingers of its front legs.

Diplodocus probably lived in herds. Fossils of Diplodocus have been found in the Rocky Mountain states.

Supersaurus and Ultrasaurus

(SOO–per–saw–rus and UHL–tra–saw–rus)

In Colorado in the 1970s, scientists found a few fossil bones of two of the largest animals that ever lived on Earth. So far the skeletons are not complete, and the animals have not been given scientific names. But the scientists gave the dinosaurs nicknames because of their size.

The first bones found were those of Supersaurus, which means "super lizard." One shoulder bone of Supersaurus was longer than a tall person. Supersaurus was probably much like Brachiosaurus. It may have been over ninety feet long and more than fifty feet tall.

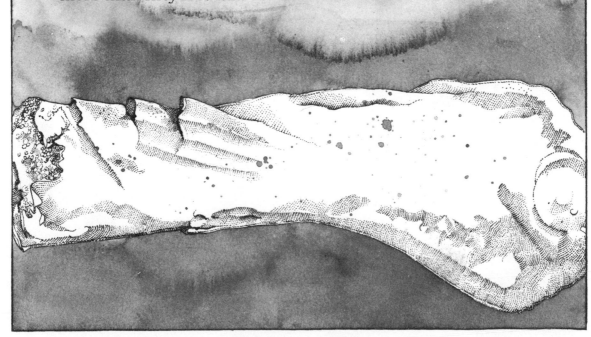

Ultrasaurus was found a few years after Supersaurus. Ultrasaurus was even larger than Supersaurus. Ultrasaurus means "ultra lizard." It may have been the largest dinosaur ever. It may have been more than one hundred feet in length. It may have stood sixty feet tall. Some scientists think it weighed more than one hundred tons. Its shoulder bone, the largest single fossil bone ever found, was nine feet long.

Both these sauropods were plant-eaters. They probably browsed on the tops of tall trees. They must have had to eat all day long to provide energy for their huge bodies.

Scientists do not know why they grew so big. Perhaps they kept growing for as long as they lived. Perhaps these two dinosaurs lived for two hundred years or more. Their huge size must have protected them from meat-eating dinosaurs.

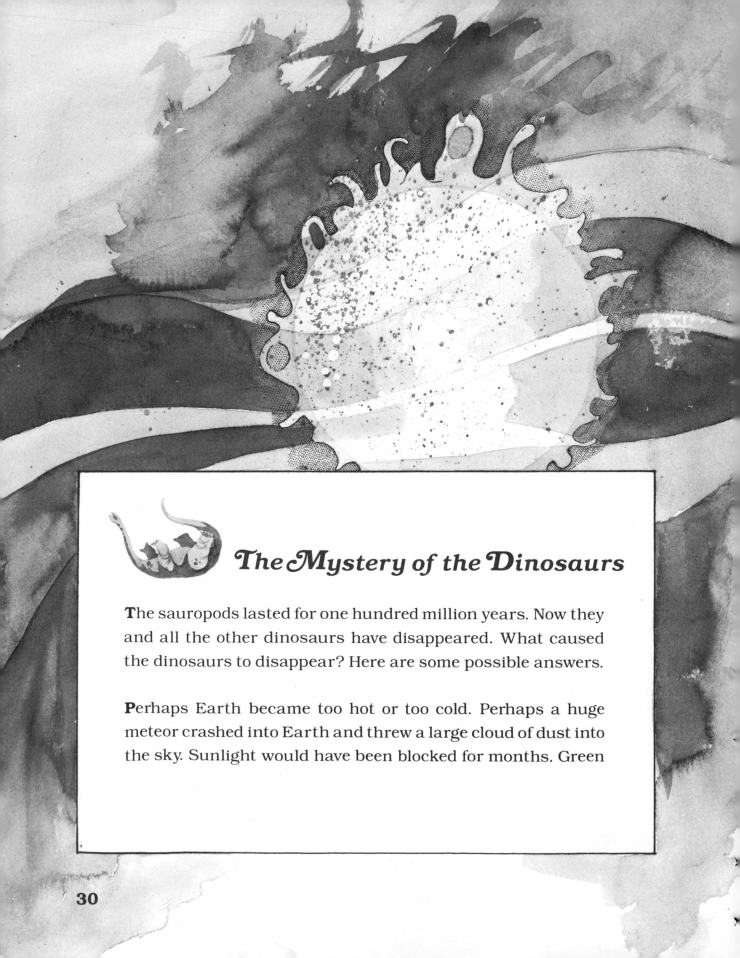

The Mystery of the Dinosaurs

The sauropods lasted for one hundred million years. Now they and all the other dinosaurs have disappeared. What caused the dinosaurs to disappear? Here are some possible answers.

Perhaps Earth became too hot or too cold. Perhaps a huge meteor crashed into Earth and threw a large cloud of dust into the sky. Sunlight would have been blocked for months. Green plants would have died, because they need light to live and grow. Then the sauropods would have died without any plants to eat. The meat-eating dinosaurs would have died without any plant-eaters to eat.

Perhaps none of these ideas are right. No one knows for sure. Why the dinosaurs disappeared may always remain a mystery.

Index